P9-DUD-220

BEST DAY EVER

by
Michael J. Armstrong

illustrated by
Églantine Ceulemans

STERLING CHILDREN'S BOOKS
New York

William's Summer Goals
1. ~~Math Camp MVP~~
2. ~~Read 50 books~~
3. ~~Hablar Español~~
4. ~~Black belt in Karate~~
5. ~~Perfect Guitar Recital~~
6. Have most fun ever.

Learn Spanish in ONE SUMMER
It's the last day of summer, and I have one final piece of business: have the most fun ever. And I'm going to measure it . . . just to be sure.

Apparently bouncing can be fun.
Bouncing BASICS

Unfortunately, it's not the most fun ever.

Hi, WILL!
I prefer William.
Do you want to bounce to the MOON and discover alien DINOSAUR bones then become WORLD-FAMOUS space paleontologists who get to ride in a parade but we won't throw any CANDY because everyone is throwing all their candy to us since we're so AWESOME?
THE MILLERS

No, thank you, Anna. I'm busy, and I don't have time for *silliness*.
You don't look busy.

Studies show that artistic expression is associated with high levels of fun.
A painting primer

Hmm, it's still not the most fun ever. This might be harder than I thought.

Look, WILLY!
William.

Do you want to ride these talking SEAHORSES to a SECRET underwater castle and RESCUE the starfish king from the WICKED SQUID WIZARD who lies all the time and needs his attitude adjusted?
Please, Anna. I'm working on something important here. Besides, you're making a mess.
What MESS?

I've noticed that these foot-powered vehicles are popular with kids today.
FUN

Rats!
Something isn't right. I should have had the most fun ever by now.
MIH?

Hey WILLY NILLY!
Do you want to jump our MOTORCYCLES across the Grand Canyon to escape from the GREEDY TOAD PIRATE who keeps trying to steal our TREASURE with his long, sticky tongue and also he smells WEIRD?
TREASURE

My name is *William*!
I'm trying to have fun!
And that's not safe. Now, *please* stop bothering me.

Oh, no! Time is wasting. I need to work harder. Think, man. Think!
What is that NOISE?

TOOT!
Excuse me, Anna. I'm trying to think. Can you please quiet down?
Nope.
Not when I'm playing with my MAGICAL MYSTERY STICK. See? It can do anything. It was a gift from the GIANT FAIRY QUEEN who lives inside the BIG ROCK CANDY MOUNTAIN and is very kind but sometimes she TOOTS by accident and causes an AVALANCHE.
ROLL ROLL

WHOA. That's odd. What exactly are you doing, Anna?

I'm having the MOST FUN EVER, of course.
THAT'S IT!
Anna, will you teach me? Will you teach me how to have the MOST FUN EVER?

Oh, I'm *very* busy doing important, busy-by-myself things.
Please, Anna? I need your help!

Are you sure? It might get SILLY.
If it must.
And MESSY.
I'll adjust.
And a tiny bit DANGEROUS.
A tiny bit?
Teeny tiny.

I accept your terms.
A wise choice, William. Now take this and follow me! The CUTE-CUTE baby penguins have been kidnapped by a giant, INTERGALACTIC SPACE TOE who is making them eat ASPARAGUS. We are their only hope!
Your turn. Go.

Yes . . . um . . . I suppose . . . um . . .
It's OK. There are no wrong answers.
Right. So, I propose that . . . SPACE TOE must be nearby.
Good.
SNIRF
Because I detect . . . THE FOUL STENCH OF DIRTY FEET!
That's it. Keep going.

There he is!!! En garde, Space Toe!
We are the STAR PATROL, protectors of the universe
who also engage in occasional, LIGHT-HEARTED PIRACY.
You shall torment the baby penguins no more.
CHARGE!!!

LOVELY PENCILS ~ BRIGHT COLORS ~
LOVELY